TWELVE GIFTS FOR
SANTA CLAUS

MAURI KUNNAS

with Tarja Kunnas
translated from the Finnish by Tim Steffa

Crown Publishers, Inc., New York

In the far-off North, where reindeer and elves live side by side, lies a snug little village.

It is the home of Santa Claus.

Like all the other elves, little Willie loved Christmas. Giving gifts was what he loved best.

But this year he couldn't decide on a gift for Santa Claus. It had to be something very special, and Christmas was only twelve days away.

All of a sudden, Willie had an idea.

"What if we make Santa happy for the next twelve days?" Willie whispered to his dog, Tyke. "Twelve surprises!"

Willie started right away.

1 Deciding on the first gift for Santa Claus was easy. Santa's library was the biggest mess in the North. Books and papers were scattered everywhere.

"I'll surprise Santa by straightening the place up a little," Willie said to Tyke.

So Willie took out the vacuum cleaner. Then he got a broom. Then he took out the mop.

"I need more than this," Willie thought. He took another mop, a feather duster, a bucket, a brush....

Soon Willie had so much stuff that he couldn't even move, let alone get through the door.

"Oh, no!" Willie said, sighing. "Now how am I going to make Santa happy?"

"Why don't you forget about cleaning?" Santa laughed. "Just go outside and play. That would make me very happy."

And that gift made Willie happy, too.

2 The next day was so cold that little Willie stayed inside. His mother and some of the other elves knitted scarves and woolen mittens for their families.

"I will knit a thick red stocking cap for Santa Claus," Willie thought. "That will make him happy today."

But as Willie was starting to work, a kitten sprang out of nowhere and jumped on the ball of yarn.

The kitten rolled to the left. He rolled to the right. The more he tried to get loose, the more he got tangled up.

"This was much easier to make than an ordinary stocking cap," Willie told Santa when he gave him his gift.

"Just what I've always wanted." Santa laughed. "A woolen cap that says *meow*!"

3 The next morning was warmer and the village schoolyard was turned into a skating rink. Everyone raced around, playing tag.

"I bet Santa would like this," Willie said to Tyke. "He should have his own place to skate."

Off Willie ran to the sauna.

Willie hauled buckets and buckets of water on his sled. And before long, the path outside Santa's workshop was a glossy, slippery sheet of ice. Willie sat down to wait.

At last Santa Claus came out. *Zaaa-whoop! Boom!*

Everyone in the workshop rushed to the door. Santa was laughing so hard that he slid in circles on the ice.

"Santa wouldn't be much good at playing tag," Willie whispered to Tyke. "He can't even stand up."

4 The next day, all the elf children gathered outside to make snow forts, snowmen, sledding hills, and snow lanterns.

Willie made a snow reindeer.

For antlers, he used branches. The eyes and mouth were coal. And his mother gave him a bright red cherry for the nose.

"It's beautiful!" Willie exclaimed. "We should take it to Santa Claus."

Santa was in the exercise room. Willie shook the snow reindeer out of the basket, but somehow it didn't look the same indoors.

Santa still thought it was a wonderful gift. Right at that moment, a bright red cherry was exactly what he wanted.

5 "Look how hard it's snowing, Tyke," Willie said. "I know how we'll make Santa happy today. We'll shovel the snow away from the front of his workshop."

The heaviest snowfall of the season was coming down. Willie shoveled with all his might until he was absolutely worn out. He had to sit down and rest a little.

Santa opened the workshop door and peeked out.

"There's little Willie's shovel, but where's Willie?" Santa said. "Break out the shovels, everyone! There's no time to lose!"

Finally, Willie's pointed red cap showed through the snowdrift.

Willie was chilled through and through, but he had a drink of hot cider and didn't even catch a cold. That made Santa very happy.

"Hee, hee... we did it again today," Willie thought.

6 Each year, the elves had a ski race. A pocketknife was the prize.

"What a gift that would make for Santa Claus," Willie thought.

The bigger children zoomed off, but one of Willie's skis stayed at the starting line.

At the half-way point, Willie drank cup after cup of soup.

Willie decided to ski as fast as he could to catch up with the other racers. But the hill must have been too steep for Willie. He went down the slope head over heels.

"Don't worry that you didn't win the pocketknife," said Santa. "I would be very happy if you gave me your skis to repair."

And of course Willie did. Especially since it made Santa Claus so happy.

7 As always at Christmastime, Santa received cards and letters by the bagful.

They came from America, Europe, and the Nordic countries. Japan, Australia, and Africa. New Zealand, Hawaii, and the Sunda islands—from every corner of the globe where there were little children.

Willie liked to sit in Santa's office and look at all the cards on the wall.

Cards
and
Letters

"I should make Santa a card of my own," Willie said. "But my card will be much bigger and more colorful than these."

Willie ran to his room.

Finally, the card was ready and Willie knocked on Santa's door.

"Such a splendid Christmas card has never been seen in this neck of the woods," Santa Claus said. "Let's leave it outside for awhile so everyone can admire it."

Willie was bursting with pride.

"By tomorrow it may even be dry," an old elf whispered to Santa with a smile.

8 During the night more snow fell. The elves worked hard keeping the walks clear.

When Willie went to the shed to fetch his plow, he overheard Santa saying, "Can it be so late already? There's not enough time to get everything done. If only the clock would slow down a little."

Willie was flabbergasted. For him, the clock moved too slowly already. There were still five long days before Christmas.

Then Willie had an inspiration.

He waited until night came to the North and everyone in Santa's village was fast asleep.

Willie crept silently down to the huge grandfather clock. It was the most important clock in the village.

Willie didn't have the slightest idea of how to slow the clock down. But he thought he had an even better plan. He stopped the clock entirely.

"Now Santa has more than enough time," he said.

Oh, the rush and commotion when the first elves woke up the next morning and found that they had overslept.

The elves were used to being awakened by the loud chiming of the clock. They couldn't understand why the clock had stopped.

But Santa guessed the reason.

"Well, for once I got enough sleep," he said.

Willie was pleased. After all, Santa was happy again.

9 That afternoon Willie baked a batch of gingerbread cookies for Santa. They looked and smelled delicious.

"Mmmm...I should taste one of the heart-shaped ones," Willie thought. "I doubt Santa will mind." And so Willie ate one.

It was so tasty that Willie just had to pop another one into his mouth.

"They are very good," he thought. And he ate a third, a fourth,
a fifth. Tyke also had a few.

Eventually, Santa came into the kitchen.

"Here you are, Santa Claus," little Willie said proudly.

"Thank you, Willie," Santa responded happily, smacking his lips. "It's been a long time since I tasted such good gingerbread crumbs."

10 Three days before Christmas the school choir performed for Santa. The choir sang a lovely Christmas carol they had rehearsed.

Santa liked it very much.

"Listen, Tyke," Willie said. "We could also play something for Santa Claus. Do you know a good song?" Tyke didn't of course. And Willie didn't either.

Then Willie remembered the brass band's old drum in the attic. Even he knew how to play that.

Santa was having a quiet evening at home in front of the fire. Willie crept up behind his rocking chair.

BIM! BAM! BOOM!

It was such a powerful performance that even Tyke was startled.

And Santa was glad to find out that he, ancient old gent that he was, could still scramble with such ease onto the mantelpiece.

11 The next morning, the children went off in search of a Christmas tree. Little Willie went along, and the tree they found was perfect.

By that afternoon, the tree was standing in the parlor.

It was such a beautiful sight that Santa had a seat to admire it. As he watched the little elves decorate the tree, Santa went off to sleep.

Willie had an idea.

When Santa woke up from his nap, he was astonished.

"Ho, ho, ho." Santa laughed. "I look even better than the Christmas tree."

And all the children thought so too.

Christmas eve finally came. Only one day remained before the great Christmas celebration. Santa and most of the elves were already half-way around the world with their bags of gifts.

Willie still had one more gift to give Santa Claus. He just had to come up with something.

He wandered back and forth while the elves who stayed behind prepared for tomorrow's celebration. But nothing came to Willie's mind.

"Well," he said. "I'm sure to come up with something during the Christmas party."

12 At last, it was Christmas day. Santa and the elves returned home. Everyone dressed in their best clothes, the parlor was decorated, and the tables were loaded with food.

Santa gave Willie a fine toy. Willie was so excited he forgot he still needed one more gift for Santa Claus.

As the elves sang and danced, Willie climbed into Santa's lap and shut his eyes.

"A tiny elf in my lap, tired out from playing—that's the best Christmas present I could have." Santa whispered to Mrs. Claus.

Then Willie remembered! "Let that be my twelfth gift," he thought.

Willie's eyes were heavy with sleep and he soon drifted off to the land of dreams as the Christmas celebration went on into the night.

The End

Published in the United States by Crown Publishers, Inc., 225 Park Avenue South, New York, New York
10003 and represented in Canada by the Canadian MANDA Group
Originally published in Finland as *12 Lahjaa Joulupukille* by Otava Publishing Company Ltd.
CROWN is a trademark of Crown Publishers, Inc.
Manufactured in Finland

Library of Congress Cataloging-in-Publication Data
Kunnas, Mauri. Twelve gifts for Santa Claus. Summary: A young elf decides to give Santa one present for each of
the twelve days preceding Christmas. [1. Elves—Fiction.   2. Santa Claus—Fiction.   3. Christmas—Fiction]
I. Title.   PZ7.K9492Tw 1988   [E]   88-7078   ISBN 0-517-56631-1

10 9 8 7 6 5 4 3 2 1

First American Edition